W9-BMF-612

"I Remember!" Cried Grandma Pinky

written by Jan Wahl • pictures by Arden Johnson

Sunday

When Grandma Pinky came to our house, she always arrived in a yellow taxi. We were on the steps, waving flags. She brought nasturtiums in a clay pot.

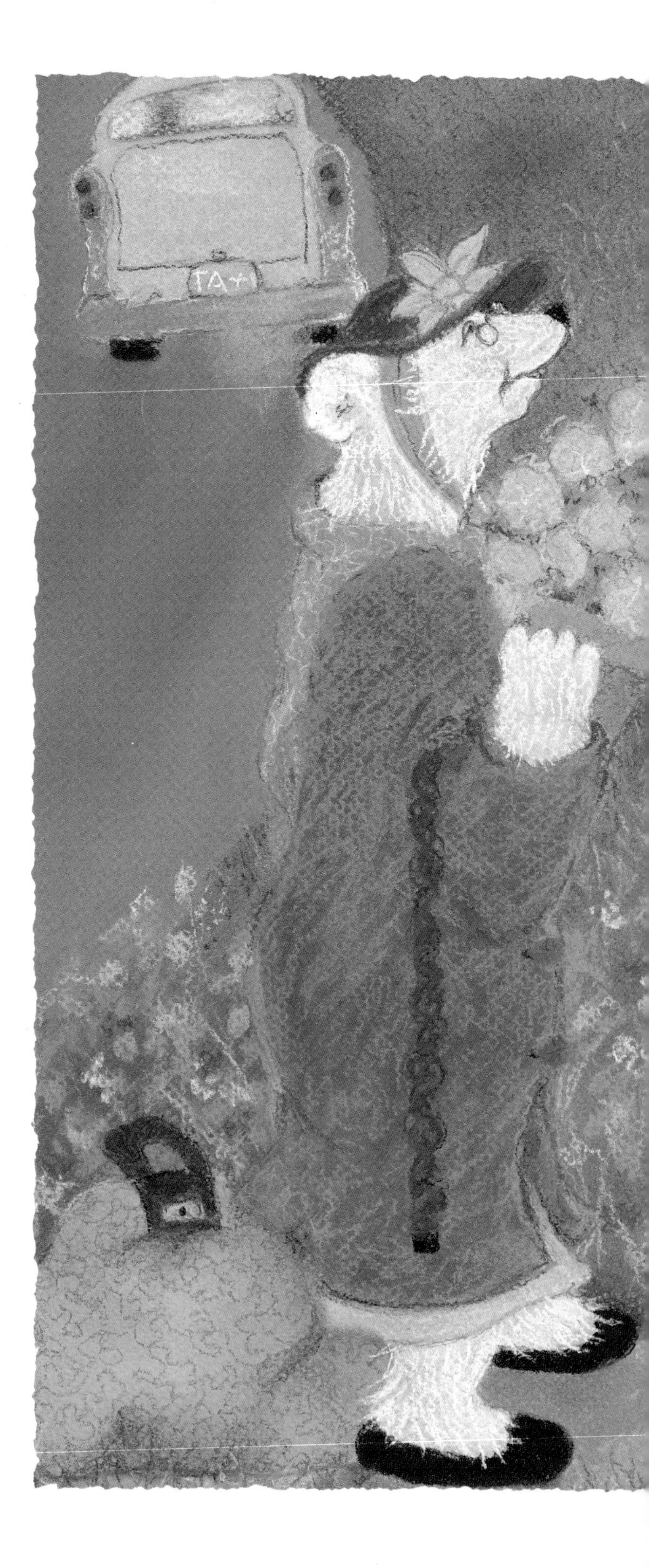

I fluffed up pillows in the best armchair.

I wanted to hear stories about what she remembered. She sat sipping cambric tea. Dunking a cracker.

"Nutmeg, I remember," she cried. "How we went berry picking one summer! I loaded a basket with black berries and red ones. We picked till it was midnight.

"My sister Clova and I did a Raspberry Hop. We wore pretty dresses. Oh, I remember so much."

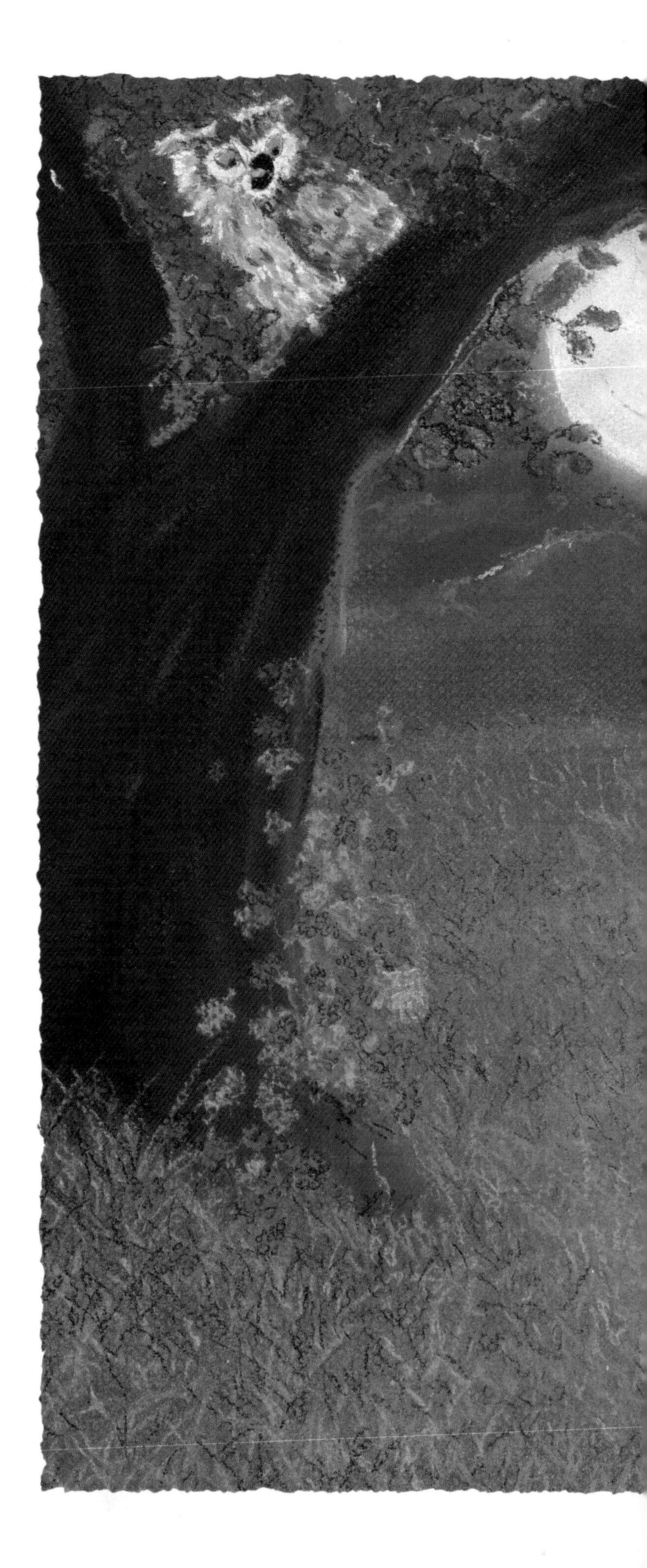

But when Grandma Pinky climbed into bed that night, she forgot her shoes, her cane, her hot water bottle, and her jar of licorice drops. I carried them up to her and almost tripped.

Her false teeth lay in a little green dish by the bed. I gave her a hug and she smiled. I ran out in the hall and giggled.

"I forgot to say good night!" she called. I knew she forgot.

Monday

It wasn't easy to get Grandma Pinky into a hammock in the back yard. But once she was there, she swung in a slow wind. On the grass, I hunted for worms.

Suddenly she looked up at the apple tree.

"I remember, I climbed a tree like that. I fell out and broke my left leg. I hobbled on crutches for weeks.

"I remember as if it were today!" she said, shaking her leg.

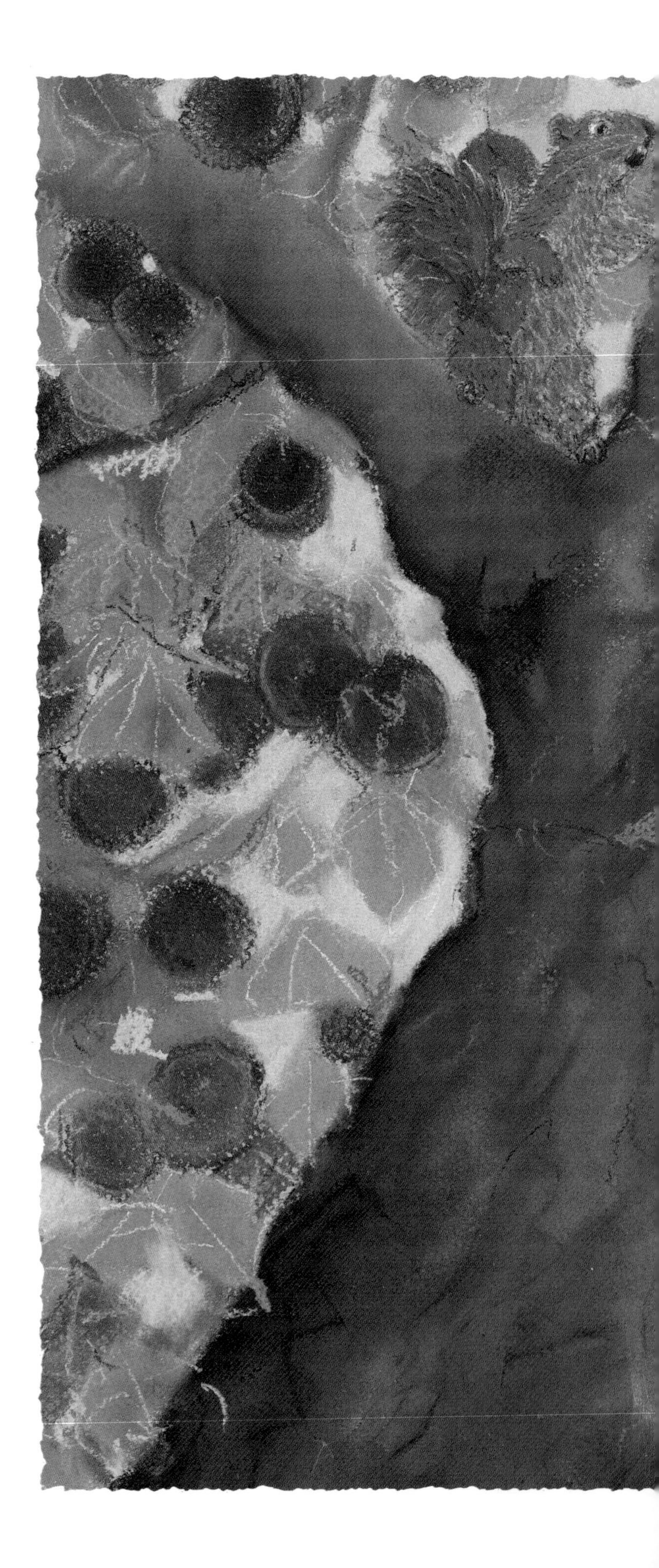

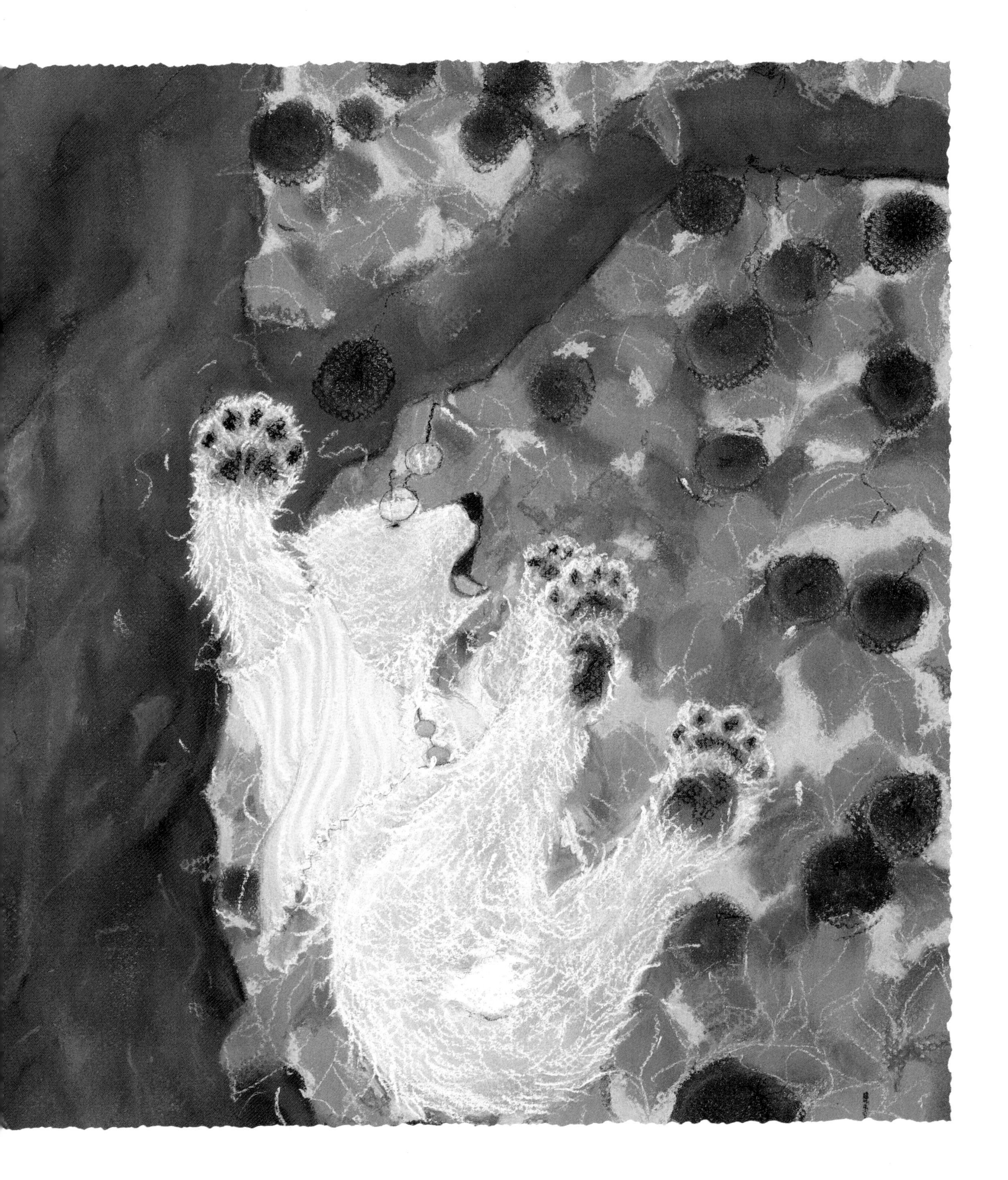

Before supper, we went walking, only Grandma and me. It took a long time just to go around the block. She stopped in front of my friend Solly's house.

"I don't remember," said Grandma, blinking her eyes. "Was it yesterday— or the day *before* — I came?"

"Yesterday," I told her. Solly waved at us from the front porch. Grandma had to go home to the bathroom.

Tuesday

I was helping Mother sweep and dust. Grandma Pinky rushed into the room. "I can't find my glasses," she declared.

She began to turn things upside down. "I don't remember where I put them!"

Mother and I both spoke together. "Grandma. You're wearing them on your nose!"

Grandma smiled sadly at us, and went away.

That night, I took a tub bath. Father shampooed me. Grandma Pinky watched from the hall.

"I remember, long ago!" she cried. "Our tin tub was in the kitchen, next to the stove. I wore a cap. I pretended I steered a ship out to sea. A red bird named Bob sat near me!"

"Grandma remembers many things," I told father.

He chuckled. "She certainly does."

Wednesday

Grandma remembered a lot. Mostly she remembered after breakfast.

We got a good game of Chinese checkers going. All at once Grandma laughed out loud. "I remember one spring," she cried. "I was sure the Easter bunny might never find me.

"So I became the bunny. I tied on ears made of cloth. When the real bunny arrived, I stared at him. He stared at me!"

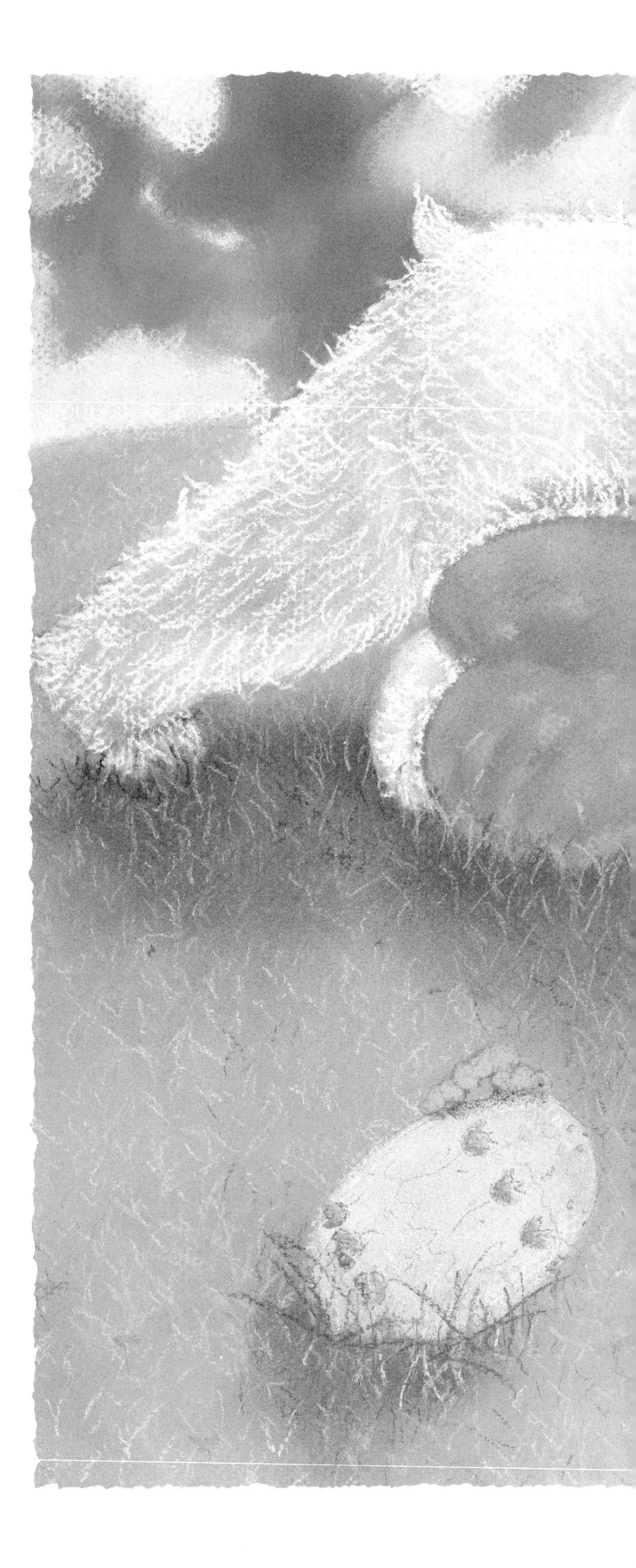

Grandma winked. "Nutmeg, how about deep dish apple pie?"

"Yippee," I yelled.

"I can make it with my eyes shut," she bragged, tying on an apron.

I brought ten nice new apples in. She sliced them with care. Grandma Pinky let me sift the flour. She added brown sugar, butter, cinnamon, and cloves.

Next she put the pie in the oven.

SUGAR

About noon, our kitchen filled with thick, black smoke. Mother hurried in. Grandma had gone to take a nap.

Mother quickly called the Fire Department. The siren was exciting. Grandma Pinky slept through the whole thing.

"She forgot her pie!" sighed Mother. That evening, Father went to the store to buy another pie. We never told Grandma.

"Great pie, Grandma," I said.

Father gave me a funny look. We ate in silence.

Thursday

I was shaking small white petals off a bush. They fell like snow on the grass. Grandma Pinky was humming to herself. A bee buzzed.

She stopped and cried:

"I remember it well! It was snowing like popcorn.

"We bundled up in sleighs, with hot bricks to keep our feet warm. WHOOSH! We raced through the hills at top speed into the woods. My sister Clova in her sleigh, me in my sleigh!

"Our horses galloped neck and neck for miles."

"Who won?" I asked.

But Grandma was asleep again.

Friday

Father mowed the lawn. I pulled out weeds. Mother was painting a fence. She went to the house to check on Grandma. She rushed back out with her fur up.

"Grandma Pinky is gone!" she called. "I looked for her everyplace!"

Father stopped pushing his mower. I dropped weeds.

"She was cutting bluebells and daisies, last," he remembered.

"But now she's lost," moaned Mother.

Quickly, the three of us tried finding her. A cool breeze blew along the street. Leaves shook above our heads. Wrens and robins worried.

"Grandma Pinky," Father shouted. "Where are you?"

At last I spotted her down the street, standing in my friend Solly's yard. Picking begonias.

"Were you lost?" Mother asked in a quiet voice.

"I was sure Nutmeg would find me," Grandma Pinky replied, holding my paw softly.

Saturday

After supper, Grandma Pinky yawned. She was tired and went up to bed.

Father hid behind the newspaper. He said, "She grows forgetful. She is growing old."

It was my turn to dry the dishes. I put down the cloth.

"But she remembers so much," I said. "I like to hear it."

Mother leaned over to give me a kiss. "Well, Nutmeg, why don't you go up and tell her that, before she sleeps?"

I raced upstairs to tell her. Grandma Pinky's lamp was still on. Her book lay open on the bed. Her eyes were shut. I would tell her tomorrow.

I was about to leave when I saw Grandma's eyes pop open.

"I remember!" Grandma began.

I smiled. "What do you remember?" I asked. And I listened until we both fell asleep.

For Craig and Suzanne - JW

To my sister, Kristen - AJ

Published by BridgeWater Books, an imprint of Troll Associates, Inc.

Printed in the United States of America.

10 9 8 7 6 5 4 3 2 1

Library of Congress Cataloging-in-Publication Data

"I Remember!" Cried Grandma Pinky / by Jan Wahl; pictures by Arden Johnson.

p. cm.

Summary: Nutmeg loves to hear Grandma Pinky tell stories about the old days, but she worries when Grandma becomes forgetful about more recent activities.

ISBN 0-8167-3456-9 (lib. bdg.) ISBN 0-8167-3457-7 (pbk)

[1. Grandmothers—Fiction. 2. Old age—Fiction. 3. Polar bear—Fiction. 4. Bears—Fiction.] I. Johnson, Arden, ill.

PZ7.W1153 1994

[E]—dc20 93-33806